THE
ISOBEL
JOURNAL

JUST A GIRL FROM WHERE NOTHING REALLY HAPPENS

THE ISOBEL JOURNAL

SWITCH
PRESS

First published in the United States in 2015
by Switch Press
A Capstone Imprint
1710 Roe Crest Drive
North Mankato, Minnesota 56003
www.switchpress.com

First published in Great Britain in 2013 by Hot Key Books
Northburgh House, 10 Northburgh Street, London EC1V 0AT

Library of Congress Cataloging-in-Publication Data

Harrop, Isobel, author.
The Isobel journal / by Isobel Harrop.
pages cm
First published: London : Hot Key Books, 2013.
Summary: Eighteen-year-old Isobel's narrative scrapbook uses mini-graphic novels, photographs, sketches, and captions to relate her witty observations about herself, friendship, and love.
ISBN 978-1-63079-003-5 (paper over board) - ISBN 978-1-63079-009-7 (eBook)
1. Scrapbooks--Juvenile fiction. 2. Teenagers--Conduct of life--Juvenile fiction. 3. Friendship--Juvenile fiction. [1. Scrapbooks--Fiction. 2. Conduct of life--Fiction. 3. Friendship--Fiction. 4. Youths' writings.] I. Title.

PZ7.H25619Is 2015
[Fic]--dc23

2014001862

Art Direction: Jet Purdie
Cover: Jan Bielecki
Interiors: Sonny Richmond, Dan Bramall
Estoy Bueno Font Credit: Denise Bentulan (douxiegirl.com)

Printed in China.
032014   008080RRDF14

ISOBEL HARROP

For everyone stuck where
nothing really happens

ME

My name is Isobel.

I live at home
with my dad

Stepmother

5-year-old
sister

2-year-old
sister

and big
brother

and our cat, Archie

UNDERWEAR SHOPPING WITH DAD =
EMBARRASSMENT

(Once I was out with my dad, and I'm not sure how or why, but he'd been walking around with a feather in his hair all day.)

I go to stay with my mom, stepdad,
and little brother a lot too!

My mom has a dog named Poppy.

I love drawing
things that I see.

I love tea

I don't want
to be one of
those people . . . but it _is_ great!

A lot of the time, I live in my own world.

Occasionally I
daydream.

I have been known to draw tattoos
on my legs with felt-tip pens.

I buy a lot of records from vintage shops.

Books!

Photographs!

I LIKE
COLLECTING
THINGS AND
STICKING
THEM IN MY
JOURNAL.

ONE

ONE

Buttons!

HOOKED ON BOOKS

Ticket stubs!

ONE

My favorite
thing to do
is probably
lying in bed
or eating
snacks . . .
or both at
the same time.

I love riding my bike . . . with the wind on my face
and in my hair and all the blood rushing around,
it is impossible to feel bad.

Sometimes I get on my bike and go
exploring around my hometown.
I like to look for secret places.

HANDS

17:44

M

1872

Merseyrail

29

WHEN RIDING YOUR BIKE IN A SKIRT, MY TOP TIP IS TO WEAR OLD EXERCISE SHORTS UNDERNEATH TO CONFUSE PASSERSBY.

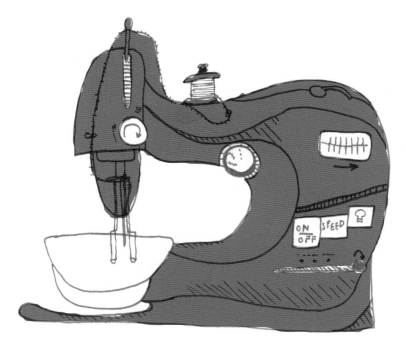

I've tried to teach myself some new skills and get some new hobbies, but I always end up either back in bed or on the computer.

Maybe I need to concentrate harder.

I WAS WALKING DOWN THE STREET
ONCE AND THIS GUY TOLD ME
"SORRY, LOVE,
YOU'VE DROPPED YOUR SMILE!"

I THINK I AM TRYING TO SAY
SOMETHING PROFOUND HERE . . .

ME IN MY NATURAL HABITAT.

Fresh sheets are so great!

Putting them on is not.

EVERY SO OFTEN I FEEL LIKE A PRINCESS.

MY DAD GIVES ME TEA IN
A PRINCESS MUG — HE
KNOWS ME TOO WELL.

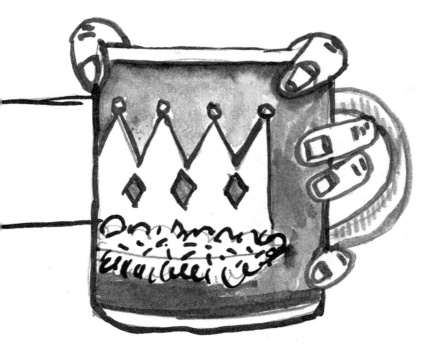

I AM IN
CHARGE OF
MY OWN
LIFE.

I like to play "Pretend I am Beyoncé."

But I wouldn't mind being
her sister, Solange, either.

I am waiting for my time to shine as a pop star.

And to discover my dark side.

I LOVE DISCOVERING NEW BANDS — IT FEELS LIKE A SPECIAL SECRET.

JUST THINKING ABOUT YOUNG
JARVIS COCKER IS TOO MUCH FOR
MY LITTLE HEART TO HANDLE.

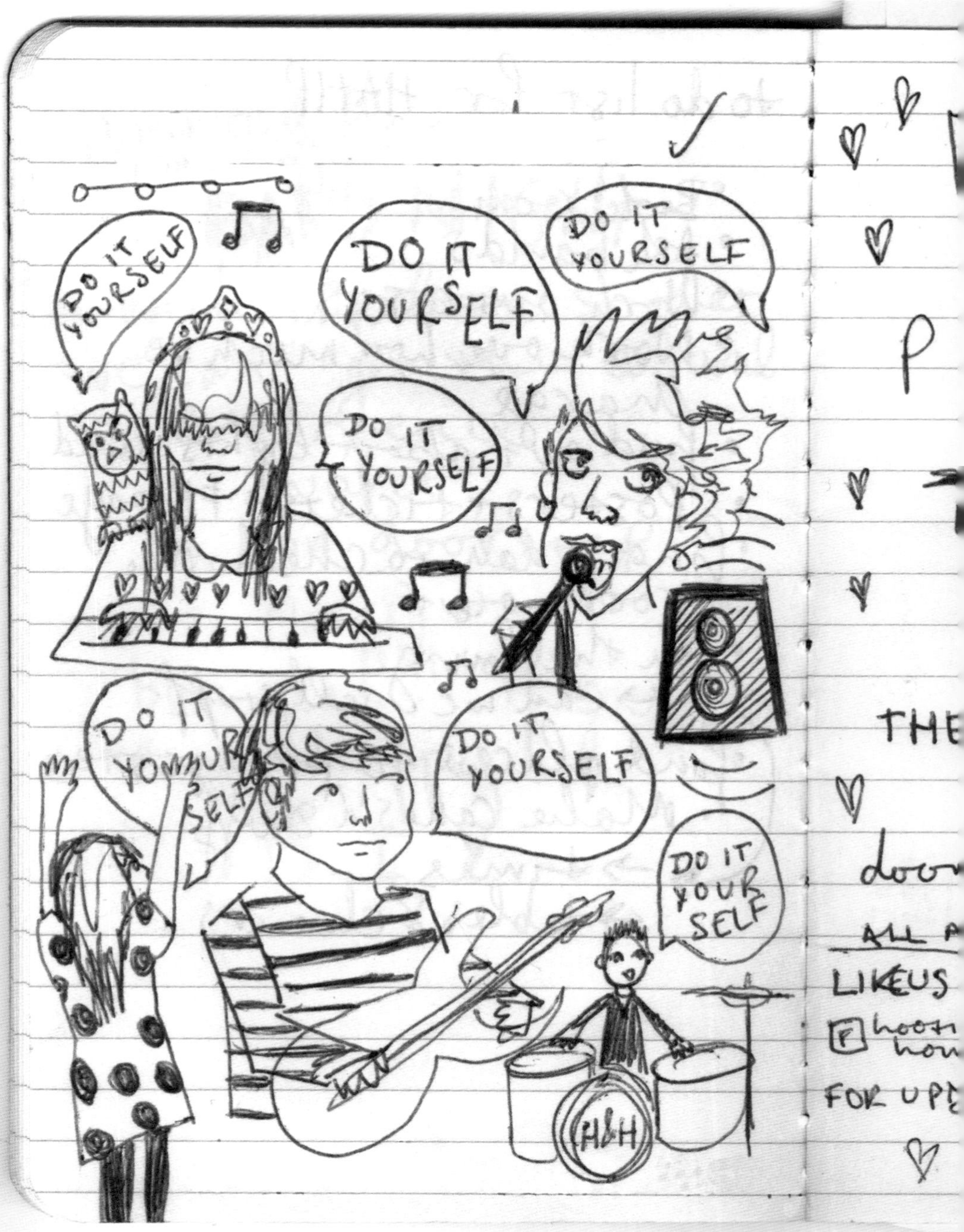

WHEN I'M QUEEN, YOU WILL BE ABLE TO WEAR TIGHTS AS PANTS!

HELLO 17th
BIRTHDAY
2/4/12
(28th April)

RED SHIRT

TIGHTS

DR-
EAM
DRESS

I guess tights are an important part of my wardrobe . . .

Hair is tricky. Having short hair is so freeing I almost want to shave it off. But people can be so rude about short-haired girls. I get lots of compliments when I have long hair, but it's a hassle! Maybe I have to find a middle ground.

Having your hair cut short is
scary at first, but then it gets
really addictive. You need to
know when to stop . . .

When I first had my hair cut short,
the hairdresser shaved my neck.
Was it abnormally hairy to begin with?

Despite everything though, sometimes I want to get my hair cut even shorter so I can be like Jean Seberg in a '60s French film.

I'm addicted to stupid
vintage clothes.

SOMETIMES I SHOULDN'T
BE ALLOWED TO DRESS
MYSELF.

ALL OF MY SHOES ARE BASICALLY A VARIATION OF ONE ANOTHER (BLACK AND STOMPY).

And I love stripes!

Sometimes I worry that people don't understand the slight irony in my love of '90s girl bands and just think I'm weird. But I guess I don't care, because "I'm A Survivor!"

And because I, uhh, listen to lots of cool indie stuff too, um, yeah . . .

FRIENDS, OTTERS, COLLEGE, & ART

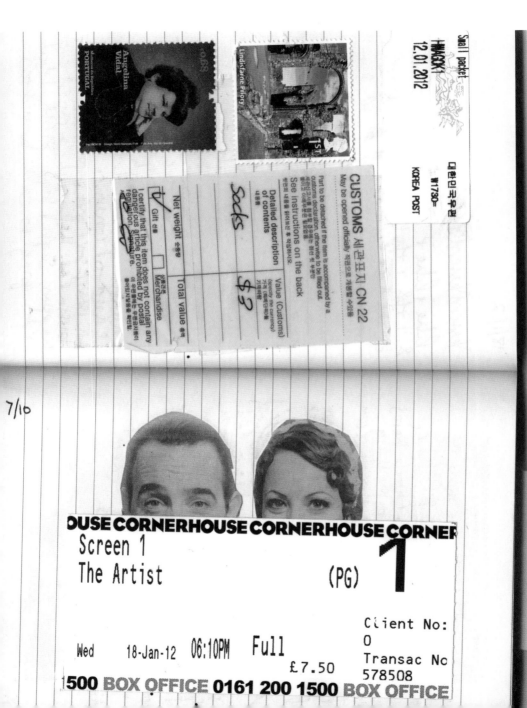

7/10

Small packet
HWAGOK1
12.01.2012

대한민국우편
₩1730=

KOREA POST

Museu da Republica
PORTUGAL
Angelina Vidal
89c

Lindisfarne Priory
1ST

CUSTOMS 세관표지 CN 22
May be opened officially 직원은 개봉할 수있음

Part to be detached if the item is accompanied by a
customs declaration, otherwise to be filled out.
세관신고서를 첨부한 경우에는 분리 부분을 절취함

See instructions on the back
뒷면의 내용을 읽어보시오 ※ 참조하시오.

CUSTOMS 세관표지 CN 22

Detailed description
of contents
내용품명

Socks

Value (Customs)
(specify the currency)
가격 (통화표시함)
내용품

$3

Net weight 순중량

Socks

Total value 총액

☑ Gift 선물
☐ 상품류
Merchandise

I certify that this item does not contain any
dangerous article prohibited by postal
regulation. Signature.
이 우편물에는 우편관계법령이
금지하는 위험물질이 들어있지
않음을 확인함. 서명

CORNERHOUSE CORNERHOUSE CORNER

Screen 1
The Artist   (PG)

1

Wed   18-Jan-12   06:10PM   Full
                                    £7.50

Client No:
0
Transac No
578508

1500 BOX OFFICE 0161 200 1500 BOX OFFICE

I just want to make
beautiful things.

I came home from school swimming
in university brochures.

ART KIDS
(me feeling out of place)

DO YOU EVER SEE THOSE SUPER
COOL LOOKING GIRLS IN THE
STREET AND YOU JUST WISH YOU
COULD MAKE THEM YOUR FRIEND —
AND THEN THEY VANISH?

THE SEASONS OF

summer

MY BEDROOM WINDOW

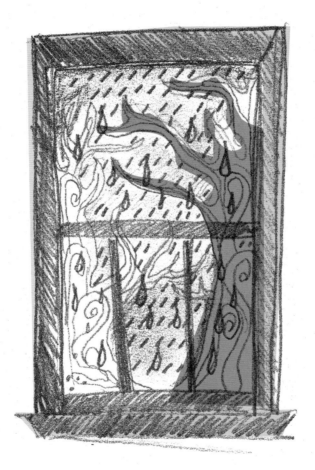

autumn

I CAN'T IMAGINE LIFE WITHOUT MY FRIENDS.

Sometimes my friend & I stand at the bus stop for ages & ages just talking about our boy problems. So much so that it has now been dubbed "boy problems bus stop."

Weekend Adventure Checklist:
Pajamas
Shower
Toothbrush
Headphones
Eyeliner
Tickets
Phone

I WISH I RAN MORE LIKE A CUTE ANIME GIRL
AND LESS LIKE PHOEBE BUFFAY.

IT'S NOT THAT I HAVEN'T
DONE MY HOMEWORK.
IT'S JUST PLAYING HARD TO GET.

I NEVER
WANT TO
DO WORK WHEN I'M
GIVEN IT, BUT WHEN I
DO SOMETHING WELL I FEEL
LIKE I'VE WON A GOLD MEDAL.

I SHOULD get a gold medal for doodling in every class.

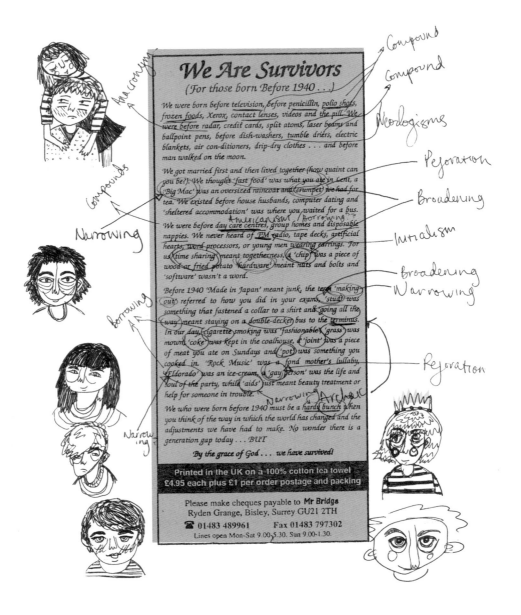

I'M NOT ANGRY HERE, I'M JUST TRYING
TO PULL OFF A MOODY-TEEN LOOK.

WATCHING ADULTS
USE THE INTERNET . . .

IS VERY, VERY PAINFUL.

I WISH I WAS A CHARACTER IN A CARTOON.

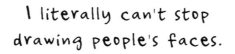

I literally can't stop
drawing people's faces.

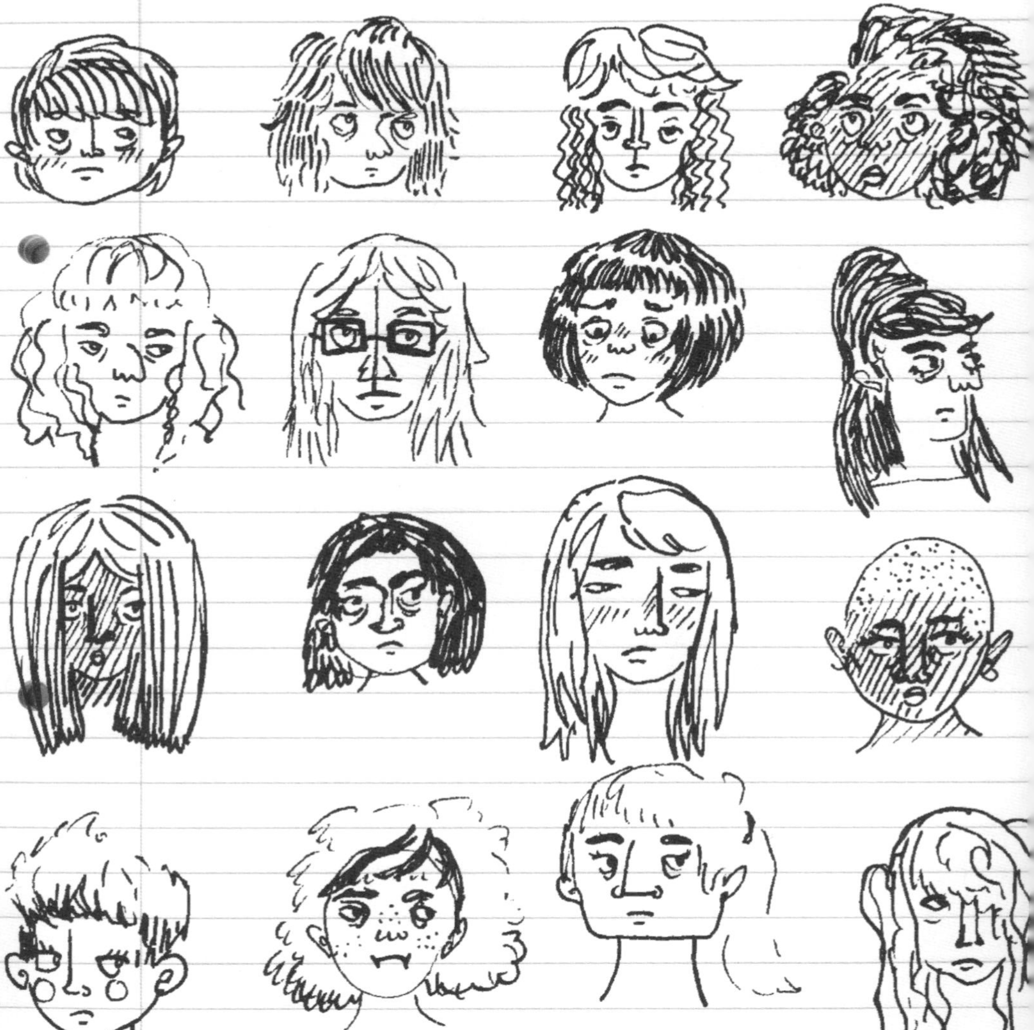

SOMETIMES PEOPLE LOOK LIKE OWLS,
AND YOU HAVE TO CAPTURE THAT.

This is an artsy "whatever" expression.

Sometimes pictures say more
than words ever can.

I went to America and drew some folks.

Ike was a guy who ran
a vintage shop and
wouldn't stop talking
to us. I felt like I had
to explain that we
don't really *do* talking
shopkeepers in the UK.

We saw Obama
talking! I copied
this from a button I
bought. His face really
is that stretchy.

THE MUSCLE MAN'S BEST FRIEND.

SASSY GIRL DRINKS SASSY SHAKE.

A COUPLE WITH CONFLICTING INTERESTS.

I wish I had half the sass of Debbie Harry.

. . . or Morrissey.

Wish you were here!

MY 'ZINE FAIR FRIEND!

LUCY C.

you triflin' good for nothin' type of brother

QUEEN OF SASS

Dear Lucy,

I hope you are well, and I hope we can see each other again soon!

Attached is:

- A CD I have been compiling for ages
- A Cath Kidston patch I bought you @ Christmas but never sent
- Dolly mixtures

I hope you like them and also your drawing.

Write back!

Miss + ♡ you

Issy

xxx xxxx xxxxx

My spirit animal is any fat,
hairy, baby animal.

I JUST CAN'T GET OVER
HOW MUCH I LOVE OTTERS.

Sea Otter

Duck-billed Platypus

DON'T BADGER THE BADGER!

Manatee

③

Tapirs

BABY tapirs!

A SLUG
IN NEED OF
A HUG

Sleepy bunnies

COYPU

SHOEBILL — THE HAPPIEST BIRD AROUND!

Pigeons are okay I guess.

But I get scared of
seagulls sometimes.

BUSHBABY

LOVE

DEDICATED TO SLEEPY BOYS.

I'M PREPARED!

I'D HAVE TO KNOW
YOU REALLY WELL BEFORE
THIS HAPPENED . . .

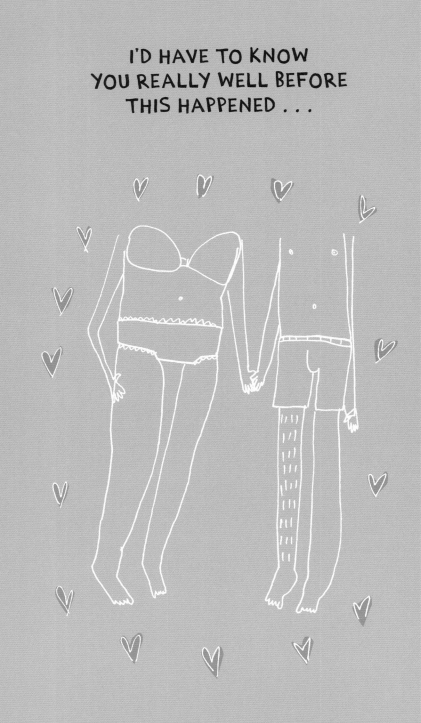

I DEMAND TO BE HUGGED.

I wish I could squish you into a tiny
ball to keep in my pocket.

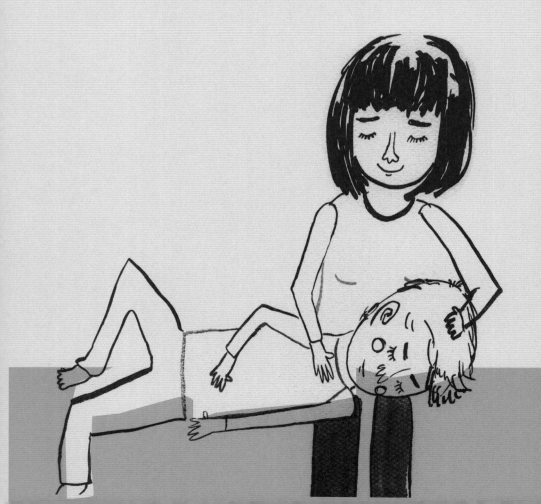

The only place to think about
deep life issues (and boys) is lying on
the bathroom floor — FACT.

SOMETIMES LOVE MAKES YOU

BEHAVE IN AN EMBARRASSING MANNER.

I'm currently revisiting my favorite teen shows from the early 2000s. And loving it.

I once thought it would be cute/funny/romantic to throw stones at a boy's window, but I threw them at the wrong one . . .

I want to plant
forget-me-nots
in your mind so that
you think about me
all the time.

I've invented a phrase which I hope all
teen girls will latch on to: boy-high.

Noun: OMG we texted all day,
I'm on a total boy-high!

The feeling you get after
Skype-ing cute boys at 3 a.m.!

I'm desperate for a part-time job.
Maybe I'll be a waitress.

A really cute one that boys
come in and write songs about.

I TRY NOT TO LET JEALOUSY TAKE ME OVER.

I'm starting to feel so close to you . . .

A winter's evening walk
is all you need for a cute date.

And fries are
the ultimate romance food.

BREAKING UP

THINGS I HATE ABOUT BOYS:

1) WHEN THEY LAUGH AT THEIR OWN JOKES AND THEY'RE NOT EVEN FUNNY

2) WHEN THEY MAKE FUN OF THE THINGS THAT YOU LIKE

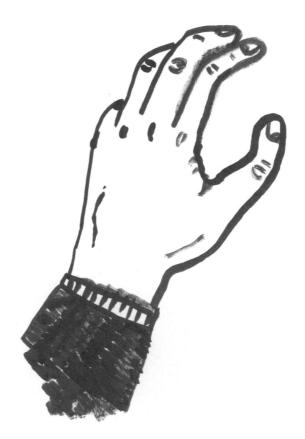

3) WHEN THEY CRACK THEIR
KNUCKLES — ALL THE TIME!

4) WHEN
THEY
SNORE
SO LOUD
YOU
CAN'T
SLEEP

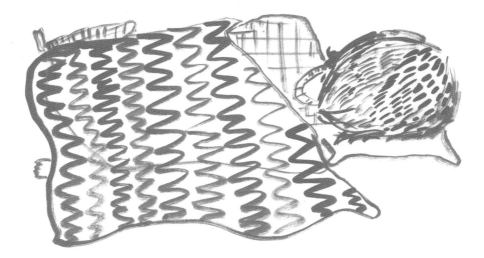

5) WHEN THEY THINK THEY'RE ENTITLED TO THE BEST SEAT

6) WHEN THEY FORGET YOUR CHRISTMAS PRESENTS

Where we fought for the first time.

I AM NOT YOUR SWEET BABOO!!!!!!!

I LIKE YOU IRONICALLY.

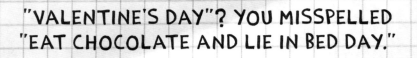

I don't believe you anymore.

I'm worried by the silence.

I THINK I PUT YOU ON TOO MUCH OF A PEDESTAL.

Sometimes I wonder when I became
too old to curl up for a cuddle when
I feel like this.

I GUESS I HADN'T EXPECTED
TO MISS YOU SO MUCH SO SOON.

I keep embarrassing myself on public transportation when I get upset about it.

Maybe I'll just sleep forever.

I'm fed up of feeling fed up.

But there will always be others,
you will always have yourself,
and your life will move on.

And things start to feel a little bit better every time I listen to "Survivor" by Destiny's Child.

It's just important to surround
yourself with good people.

ACKNOWLEDGEMENTS

First and foremost I must thank everyone at Hot Key Books for the opportunity to make this book a reality. Emily Thomas, most of all, for plucking an awkward sixteen-year-old out of northern-town obscurity and bringing her to London for what feels like the chance of a lifetime. Also Naomi Colthurst for her patience and support throughout everything and for her cute animal pictures. To Jet and Jan, the design team, for the hours of work they put in taking my schoolbook doodles and turning them into something wonderful. Of course, thank you to everyone else too, but I haven't got time to name you all! One thing I will say is that I could not have done this project with anybody else. I am tremendously lucky to know and be involved with you all; I can't put into words what a great environment Hot Key Books is — supportive kind, creative, funny, brilliant. So much love.

Secondly, of course, I want to thank my family: Dad, Justine, James, Emily, Lottie, Mom, Tony, Sam, and all the grandparents etc. etc., for being lovely at all times. Special mention to my dad for taking me down on that first 6 a.m. bus trip, for being constantly supportive, and an artistic inspiration from the beginning. Plus to my cat, Archie, for being a good cat.

Thanks to all my friends: Abi, Ashley, Maz, Fletcher, et al., you know who you are, plus everyone at school who didn't believe this was a real book; here it is. Sorry I was too shy to talk about it. And thanks most of all to Calum, for the place to stay whenever I had a meeting in London, and for always being there with *The Simpsons,* some chocolate cake, and an R. Kelly song, when I felt worn out.

A side note to thank everyone who has followed me on Tumblr and Twitter for the past few years and for putting up with my self-indulgent moaning for so long — it meant a lot.

To Mrs. Norman, for being a great teacher and an inspiration, plus everyone else at Penketh who has taught me or got to know me.

To Laura Dockrill, for her ridiculous kindness which overwhelmed me (as a huge fan) and to all those whom I have met or been involved with working on this journal.

And finally to you, for taking the time to pick up and read my jumbled teenage thoughts.

Thank you.

Isobel

Isobel Harrop is an eighteen-year-old girl from the North of England, squished somewhere between Manchester and Liverpool. She recently finished college, where she studied English Literature, English Language, and Media Studies. Now she's down in the South of England, studying English Literature "somewhere a bit more interesting." This is her first book that wasn't made using the school photocopier and staples. Inspired by *Peanuts* comics and 1960s design, Isobel loves to draw whenever she gets a chance, and almost every piece of her schoolwork is scrawled all over with drawings of imaginary people. When she isn't working or drawing, you might find her fawning over cute animals on the Internet (especially sea otters!), eating vast amounts of chocolate in all its forms, and collecting stuff that she doesn't need from vintage shops.

Follow Isobel at: www.wastingspacetime.blogspot.co.uk
or on Twitter: @IsobelJournal